A NOTE TO PARENTS

Hospitalization for a child need not be a traumatic experience. Preparing child for hospitalization by openly discussing what to expect and familiarizing the child with the hospital environment can do much to alleviate the anxieties he or she may be feeling—anxieties that are usually worse than reality.

This book is for parents and children to share together. The degree to which you as a parent can calmly participate in your child's experience can be extremely important.

—Paul Harris, M.D.
Director, Pediatric Primary Care Center
Bronx Municipal Hospital Center
Jacobi Hospital, New York City

A VISIT TO THE

CTW
SESAME STREET
HOSPITAL

A Random House PICTUREBACK®

A VISIT TO TH

With special thanks to
Dr. Judith A. Turow, M.D., and
Dr. Victor Turow, M.D., F.A.A.P.,
for their helpful advice
and suggestions
in writing this book.

Library of Congress Cataloging in Publication Data:
Hautzig, Deborah. A visit to the Sesame Street hospital. (A Pictureback book) SUMMARY: Grover visits the hospital to find out what to expect when he goes to have his tonsils out. 1. Children's stories, American. [1. Hospitals—Fiction. 2. Medical Care—Fiction. 3. Tonsillectomy—Fiction. 4. Puppets—Fiction] I. Mathieu, Joseph, ill. II. Title. PZ7.E446Vi 1985 [E] 84-17852 ISBN: 0-394-87062-X (trade); 0-394-97062-4 (lib. bdg.)
Manufactured in the United States of America 1 2 3 4 5 6 7 8 9 0

HOSPITAL

SESAME
STREET
HOSPITAL

by Deborah Hautzig • illustrated by Joe Mathieu

FEATURING JIM HENSON'S SESAME STREET MUPPETS

Random House / Children's Television Workshop

One morning Grover woke up feeling sick. "Mommy, I have a sore throat again," he whispered.

"Oh, poor Grover!" said his mother. "You have had so many sore throats this year. We will go to see Dr. Keats later today."

That afternoon Dr. Keats examined Grover. "I think your tonsils will have to come out, Grover. Then maybe you won't get so many sore throats."

Grover was worried. "How will you take them out?" he asked.

"You will have an operation. You will be in the hospital for a few days," Dr. Keats told him.

"I do not want to go to the hospital!" said Grover. "I want to stay home with Mommy!"

"Your mother can go with you. She can even stay overnight there," said Dr. Keats. "Would you and some of your friends like to visit the hospital before you go for the operation, just to see what it is like?"

Grover thought that was a good idea.

The next week Grover's mother took Grover, Ernie, and Bert to visit the hospital. Nurse Spinner was their guide.

"Wow, this is a big place!" said Ernie. "Is everyone here to have tonsils out?"

"No," said Nurse Spinner. "People come to the hospital for lots of reasons. Sometimes they need extra help to get well— special treatments or medicine that they can get only in a hospital. And many people come for a special operation, like you will have, Grover."

As they walked down the hall, Bert asked, "What's that funny smell?"

Nurse Spinner said, "You are smelling disinfectant. Hospital floors are washed with disinfectant several times a day. That's because hospitals have to be very clean all the time."

Nurse Spinner took them upstairs. "Children stay in their own section of the hospital, called the pediatric ward," she explained. "This is where you will stay, Grover.

"Most of the rooms are for two or more children. Every bed can be raised up or down at the back and front. You can sit up in bed to draw pictures or watch TV and, of course, to eat meals."

"What if I do not like the food?" asked Grover shyly. "Do I have to eat it anyway?"

"No," said Nurse Spinner. "There is a menu so you can pick something you do like! And if you want some juice or fruit between meals, just push this nurses' call button."

"What will happen if I push it?" asked Grover.

"Try it and see!" said Nurse Spinner.

Grover pushed the button.

In a few seconds another nurse came into the room.

"You sure came fast when Grover pushed that button!" said Ernie. "Where did you come from?"

"From the nurses' station. I'll show you," the nurse said.

"Every floor has a nurses' station," she went on. "It's a sort of headquarters for nurses and doctors. All the patients' charts are kept there. Your chart has all sorts of information about your medical history and daily notes made by the doctors and nurses who take care of you while you are here. When your own doctor comes to see you, he will look at your chart before he examines you."

She introduced the resident doctor. "There is always a doctor on the
floor," she explained. "When Dr. Klinger goes home, another doctor will
come to take her place."

"Now I want to show you our playroom," said Nurse Spinner. "We have blocks...crayons...paints...paper...dolls...stuffed animals...."

"Nurse Spinner," said Grover, "when I come to the hospital, may I please bring my own teddy bear?"

"Of course, Grover! And when you are well enough to get out of bed and come to the playroom, you can introduce him to *our* teddy bear!"

"Grover, this is Jane," said Nurse Spinner. "Jane had *her* tonsils out two days ago."

"Did it hurt?" Grover asked Jane.

"No, not when they took them out," said Jane. "But my throat was pretty sore after I woke up. I could only eat ice cream and Jell-O. It feels a lot better now!"

Grover felt better already.

"Wow, I love ice cream!" said Ernie. "I wonder how my tonsils are."

Bert asked Jane a question too. "What is that bracelet on your arm?"

"My hospital bracelet!" Jane said. "Everybody who stays in the hospital gets one. It has my name and a secret code number on it. All the doctors and nurses know who I am even when I am asleep, just by reading my bracelet."

The x-ray machines were next on the tour. Nurse Spinner told them that x-ray machines are like big cameras, but they use a special kind of film. "They take pictures of your bones!"

Ernie said, "Remember, Bert, I had an x-ray picture taken when I hurt my foot? The x-ray showed that my foot was not broken!"

Then they went with Nurse Spinner to the room where surgeons get ready to operate. She introduced them to one of the surgeons, Dr. Lamb.

"Why are you wearing pajamas?" Ernie asked the doctor. "Do you sleep here?"

"No," said Dr. Lamb. "This suit is part of the special clothing that we wear when we operate."

"We also wear a cap and mask," said Dr. Lamb as he put them on.

Ernie giggled. He thought the doctor looked silly in the cap and mask.

Then Bert asked the doctor why he wore a mask. "Don't you want anyone to know who you are?"

Dr. Lamb laughed. "No," he said, "we wear masks just to keep germs off the patients. We scrub our hands in special soap that kills germs. We have to be very clean. Then we put on sterile rubber gloves—sterile means germ free. And after that we put on sterile surgical gowns. Then we are ready to operate. Who would like to try on a surgical gown?"

"Me!" answered Grover and Ernie and Bert. Nurse Spinner helped them put on the gowns.

"Now I know what to be for Halloween next year!" said Ernie.

"This is the operating room, where the doctor will take out your tonsils, Grover," said Nurse Spinner. "It has an operating table, big bright lights, lots of sterile instruments, and many special machines. The machines will keep track of your breathing, blood pressure, and other important things during the operation.

"After the operation is over you will be taken to the recovery room, where you will wake up. It's just down the hall. The doctors and nurses there wear special clothes too."

"How long will I have to stay in the recovery room?" Grover asked.

"Only for a few hours," said Nurse Spinner. "When the doctors and nurses think you're ready, you'll be taken back to your room."

"Gee," said Ernie. "Doctors and nurses have to know a lot!"

"Yes, they do," said Nurse Spinner. "But sometimes they ave questions too. That is why every hospital has a medical brary. Doctors and nurses use it to find answers in books."

Grover said, "I love books! When I am in the hospital, may go to the library?"

"You won't have to," Nurse Spinner said. "A special library ill come to you on a big cart! You can check out a book right rom your bed."

"Gee," said Grover. "The hospital is not scary like I thought would be."

"Sometimes a hospital is a *very* happy place," said Nurse pinner. "I will show you the happiest part of all."

Nurse Spinner took them to the nursery. Grover looked through the glass window at the newborn babies.

"Ohhhhhhh, they are so cute," he said softly. "Was I that cute when I was a baby, Mommy?"

Grover's mother said, "You were the cutest baby of all!"

"This is the end of our tour," said Nurse Spinner.

"What's that?" asked Ernie, pointing to a window filled with toys and books.

"That's the gift shop," said Grover's mother. "Sometimes, when people are sick, their friends bring them gifts to cheer them up."

"Mommy, do you think anybody will bring me a present when I am in the hospital?" asked Grover.

Grover's mother smiled. "Oh, I think maybe someone will," she said.

Everybody thanked Nurse Spinner for a wonderful tour.

Bert said, "You were right, Nurse Spinner. The nursery is the best thing about the hospital."

Ernie said, "I think the playroom is the best."

Everybody waved good-bye to Nurse Spinner.

"Mommy," whispered Grover, "I think the best thing about the hospital is getting well!"